To
Dad and
Betsy, for
teaching me to love
nature. Even the bugs.
—B. S.

To the biscuit,
Love from the potato
—J. P.

FLAMINGO BOOKS
An imprint of Penguin Random House LLC, New York

First published in the United States of America by Flamingo Books, an imprint
of Penguin Random House LLC, 2022
Text copyright © 2022 by Becky Scharnhorst
Illustrations copyright © 2022 by Julia Patton

Flamingo Books & colophon are registered trademarks of Penguin Random House LLC.

Visit us online at penguinrandomhouse.com.

Library of Congress Cataloging-in-Publication Data is available.

Manufactured in China

ISBN 9780593403334

10 9 8 7 6 5 4 3 2 1

TOPL

Edited by Cheryl Eissing. Design by Ellice M. Lee. Text set in Litterbox ICG.
The art was done in mixed traditional and digital media.

This Field Trip Stinks!

Words by
BECKY SCHARNHORST

Pictures by
JULIA PATTON

FLAMINGO BOOKS

September 28th

Dear Diary,

This morning, Mr. Grizzly announced we're taking a field trip. I thought we'd study stars at the Planetarium or dinosaurs at the Natural History Museum. But we're going to study plants and animals . . . IN THE WILD!

Everyone was excited.
Everyone except ME!
I've read enough books to know nature is FULL of
poisonous plants, creepy crawlies, and ferocious beasts!

P.S. Isn't our class wild enough?

NATURE UNCOVERED

INTO THE WILD

CHOMP!

BYE BYE

PERMISSION SLIP

PERMISSION SLIP

WILDWOOD ELEMENTARY
FIELD TRIP. PARENT OR
GUARDIAN SIGN BELOW

September 29th

Dear Diary,

I tried losing my permission slip, but it

didn't work

I guess I have to go.

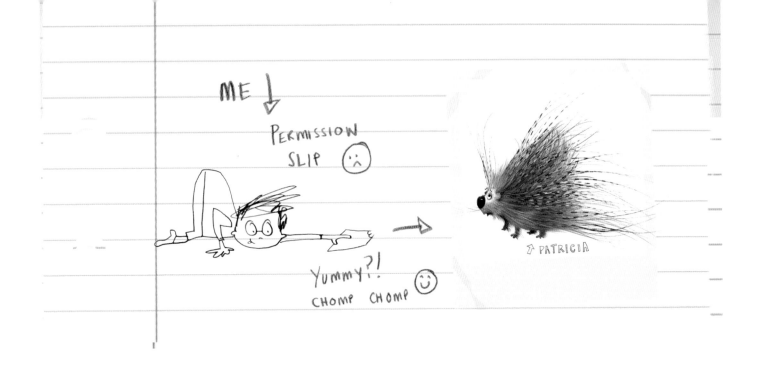

Dear Diary,

Today is our field trip.

Mr. Grizzly said we should document everything we see, so I brought you with me. Along with sunscreen, bug spray, a mosquito net, compass, water bottle, and **2 First did kits.** →

Wildwood

to the WOODS →

WILD BEARS

I also packed some HAPPY THOUGHTS.

P.S. I'm sure everything will be fine, right, Diary?

CAUTION
POISON IVY

Dear Diary,

EVERYTHING IS NOT FINE!!!

As soon as I stepped off the bus, I identified my first plant.

Charlie helped me put on anti-itch cream while everyone
else headed to the pond.
Maybe I should have brought ⌐3⌐ First did kits. → OUCH!

Dear Diary,

By the time we got to the pond, everyone was already identifying their specimens.

Charlie found tons, but he accidentally swallowed them. I didn't find any.

P.S. Mr. Grizzly said I don't count as a specimen. →

CHARLIE

SPECIMEN

ME ←

POND

Dear Diary,
After studying animal homes in nature,
we built our own shelters.

Turns out I'm not very good at it.

Dear Diary,
After it stopped raining, we divided into teams to create our own food chains.

Everyone found a food source except me.

Charlie told me not to feel bad. He said I could pretend to be his food source.

chew
chew

P.S. That didn't make me feel any better.

yum
yum

chomp
chomp

3 THINGS I HATE ABOUT NATURE FIELD TRIPS:

1. The bugs

2. The bathroom

3. DID I MENTION THE **BUGS!!?**

P.S. This field trip **STINKS**

The bathroom is that way!

But there's no toilet paper.
Or toilet.

Dear Diary,

I thought things might get better once we started birdwatching. I was wrong.

Really, really wrong.

bird
☒ poop

birds ☑

Me ☑

I told Mr. Grizzly I left my lunch on the bus, and I should probably go back and get it

RIGHT NOW!

But Mr. Grizzly said he'd share his lunch with me. I wonder if he eats peanut butter and jelly.

Dear Diary,

He DOES NOT eat peanut butter and jelly!

P.S. On the bus ride home, Charlie and I decided to have a campout.

But only in the backyard.

That's **WILD** enough for now.

Wildwood Elementary

3 things I love about nature field trips:

1. Butterflies
2. Great views everywhere, even in the bathroom
3. Being wild with my best friends

Dear Diary,

On the hike back, we snacked on blueberries and watched the sun set.

Betsy chiseled me a cool hiking stick to thank me for leading our group out,

and Mr. Grizzly gave me an **A+** in navigation.

I realized I knew the way back to the bus!

P.S. Deep breaths really **DO** help!